Zeb's Safe Bus Ride To School

Dedication

Dedicated to our amazing bus drivers,
who transform steering wheels into magic wands of safety,
guiding precious cargo through rain and shine.
To the children, whose trust and bright smiles
make every stop worthwhile,
turning ordinary routes into adventures.
To the parents, who place their most precious gifts in our care,
greeting us with waves and grateful nods
at corners and curbsides across our community.
To every member of our transportation family -
the mechanics keeping engines humming,
safety trainers sharing wisdom,
and fellow dispatchers coordinating countless journeys.
But most of all, this story celebrates
the special bond between our drivers and their young
passengers.
It's a bond built on morning greetings,
afternoon goodbyes,
shared stories and silly songs,
watchful eyes and caring hearts,
and all the small moments in between
that make a bus ride so much more
than just a journey from here to there.
It's a celebration of the everyday heroes
who make the wheels on our buses
go 'round and 'round with purpose and pride.

To every child who steps aboard our yellow buses: you are the reason we do what we do. To every driver who opens those doors each morning: you are the guardians of countless stories. The keepers of safe passages and the true heroes of our roads. May this book remind us all that sometimes the biggest adventures happen on the most ordinary routes, and the bravest heroes wear uniforms of blue and smiles of gold.?With gratitude and pride, Gloria Sanders-William

At the corner of Elm Street, where the big oak tree stood tall, children gathered at their bus stop. Among them was Zeb, bouncing on his toes, his rocket ship backpack jiggling. Today was show and tell day! In his hands, he held Rex, his favorite toy dinosaur, ready to share with his class.

Zeb heard his mom's morning words echo in his mind: "Safety first, adventure second!" Taking a deep breath, he made his excited feet stay still, even though they wanted to jump and stomp just like his dinosaur Rex would.

The big yellow bus rounded the corner, its engine humming like a friendly dragon. As it slowed down, the brakes squeaked like a giant mouse.

The big red stop sign unfolded like a flag waving hello. Zeb stood still and counted in his head, just like Ms. Joy taught them:

One Mississippi, Two Mississippi, Three Mississippi, Four Mississippi, Five Mississippi..

Only when the door swooshed open did Zeb and his classmates step forward. they gripped the handrail tight, just like holding Rex's tail.

Ms. Joy smiled warmly, "Good morning, Safety Scout Zeb! Are you ready for another safe journey to school?"

"Good morning, Ms. Joy!" Zeb smiled brightly. He carefully slipped Rex into his rocket ship backpack, making sure his friend would be safe until show and tell time.

Zeb walked carefully to his favorite seat, holding rex close. He knew running or pushing wasn't allowed—it could make the bus trip bumpy for everyone, like a dinosaur stampede!

Zeb sat straight and tall in his seat, remembering Ms. Joy's golden rules. "Be still like a watchful T-Rex," he whispered. "Use a quiet voice like a gentle Brontosaurus." He tucked his feet in close, keeping the aisle clear, and listened carefully for Ms. Joy's instructions.

All of a sudden, over the noise of the big yellow bus, a loud THUD echoed through the aisle. The chattering voices fell silent. Zeb and his classmates turned their heads toward the sound.

There, sprawled in the middle of the aisle was Molly from Mrs. Reed's Class.
The Bus swayed as Ms. Joy slowed down the bus. Molly pushed herself up, her eyes puffy from crying.
This was exactly why Ms. Joy's rules were so important.

O uch!" Molly said. She wasn't moving. The other kids looked worried. They knew their friend might be hurt. "Don't move, Molly!" Sara said, who sat in the seat right behind her. Everyone remembered what Ms. Joy taught them about safety.

"**M**s. Joy," Michael said in his inside voice, "I think Molly needs help. She fell and isn't getting back up.

Everyone knew this was an emergency and even though they were excited and worried for Molly they kept their voices down as Ms. Joy carefully pulled over to a safe spot. She quickly checked on Molly and then used her radio to call for help.

Zeb and his classmates sat still, watching
as flashing lights appeared and parked
next to the school bus.

The paramedics arrived quickly and smiled at the children. "You're all being such great helpers!" said the paramedic with the medical bag. "Staying in your seats keeps everyone safe while we help Molly."

As the paramedics checked on Molly, Ms. Joy gathered her students close. "I'm so proud of you all," she said warmly. "You remembered our safety drills and stayed calm during the emergency. Because of your quick thinking, we got Molly the help she needed."

Once Molly was taken care of and on her way to check her ankle, the bus continued its journey to school.

When they finally reached school, Zeb felt proud. He and his classmates had helped keep everyone safe on their morning ride.

Ms. Joy gave Zeb a special "super safe student" sticker, and he knew he would have another great story to add at show and tell.

LEARN MORE

My School Bus Safety Checklist
My Important Numbers

I know my Student
Number:_____
My Bus Number: _____
My Bus Route Number: _____
My Bus Number: _____
Morning Pick-up Time: _____
Afternoon Drop-off Time: _____

SAFETY SPOTS

I know where the first aid kit is located
on my bus: _____
I know my safe waiting spot at my bus
stop: _____
I know my safe meeting place if there's
an emergency: _____
I know how to open the emergency
exit door: _____
I know where all emergency exits are
on the bus: _____
I know my bus driver's name:

_____

IMPORTANT INFORMATION

My Home Address:

_____

My School's Name:

_____

My Bus Stop Location:

_____

EMERGENCY CONTACTS

My Parent/Guardian's Name:

_____

Phone Number:

_____

Second Emergency Contact:

_____

Phone Number:

_____

My School's Phone Number:

_____

Bus Rules I Promise to Follow

I will stay seated when the bus is moving: _____

I will keep the aisle clear: _____

I will use my inside voice: _____

I will keep my hands and belongings inside the bus: _____

I will follow my bus driver's instructions: _____

Remember

Stars

S - Stay calm

T - Tell an Adult if you need help.

A - Always listen to Instructions.

R - Remain in your seat.

S - Safe choices - save lives.

THE BUS SAFETY RAINBOW

- **Red:** Stop, look, and listen
- **Orange:** Wait your turn
- **Yellow:** Be careful
- **Green:** Help others
- **Blue:** Stay calm
- **Purple:** Be respectful

DAILY SAFETY CHECK
(Visual Guide)

Morning:
Look both ways
Walk to bus
Use handrail
Find seat

SAFETY RULES - ON THE BUS - I CAN HELP

If I see someone... Standing up:
Remind them to sit down

Blocking aisle: Ask them to move

Being loud: Use "quiet please" signal

Feeling sick: Tell Bus Driver

Dropping items: Wait to pick it up safely

Being bullied: Report to an adult

B - b - Bus

WORD SEARCH

B	U	S	S	A	F	E	T	Y
R	A	I	L	I	N	G	S	J
S	E	A	T	B	E	L	T	O
Q	U	I	E	T	L	C	O	Y
D	R	I	V	E	R	S	P	S
K	I	N	D	N	W	S	S	U
H	E	L	P	E	R	S	O	S

```
B S T O P S I G N A L S R W K
U E B U C K L E U P T Y U H N
S A W A L K I N G A R E A D G
D T C R O S S I N G R H L R B
R B H A N D R A I L S I E I U
I E A R U L E S T O P V S V S
V L I N E U P Q W X Y E M E D
E T R A F F I C L I G H T R R
R S L O W D O W N B Z K M S I
S I T D O W N M N O P Q R S V
F L A S H I N G L I G H T S E
Y E L L O W B U S W X Y Z A R
```

Words to Find:

BUCKLE UP   **CROSSING AREA**   **DRIVER**   **FLASHING LIGHTS**
HANDRAILS   **LINEUP**   **RULES**   **SITDOWN**   **SLOWDOWN**
STOPSIGNALS   **TRAFFIC LIGHT**   **WALKINGAREA**
YELLOWBUS

My School Bus Safety Pledge

I, _____, promise to:

Use the _____ when boarding the bus.

Stay in my _____ until the bus stops.

Use my _____ voice

Keep the _____ clear.

Listen to the _____ for Instructions.

Student Signature: _____

Date: _____

Answer Key:
handrail
seat
inside
aisle
Bus Driver

COLOR TIME

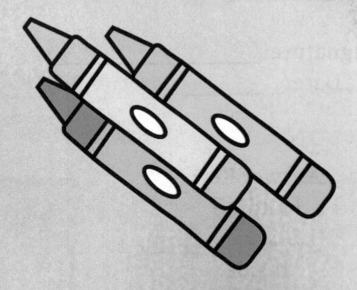

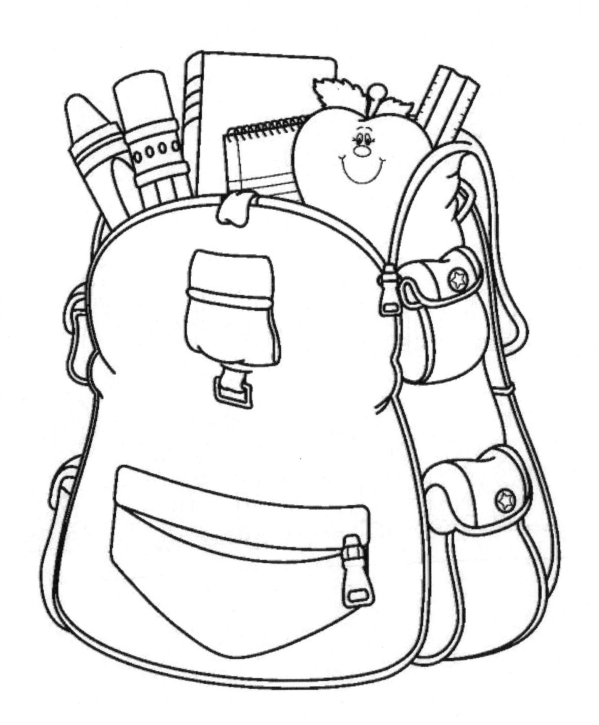

School bus

I FOLLOW THE BUS RULES TO KEEP ME SAFE

1. Light blue
2. Yellow
3. Red
4. Brown
5. Orange
6. Dark blue
7. White
8. Green
9. Grey

COLOR SOME FUN STUFF

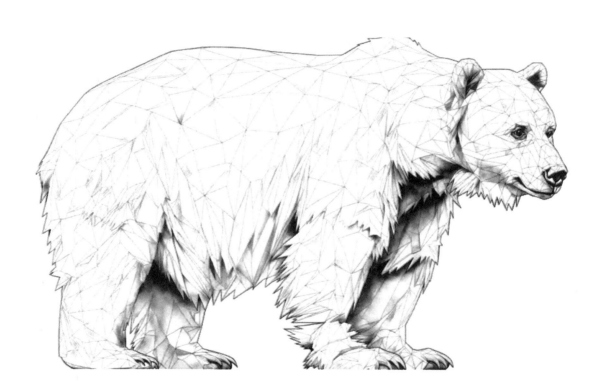

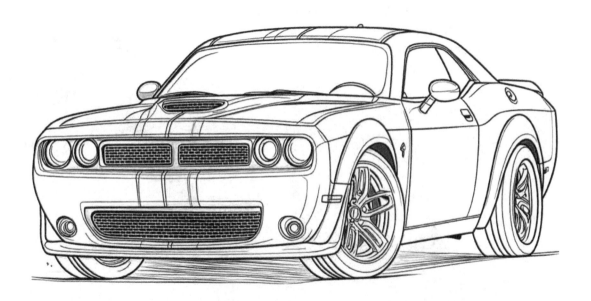

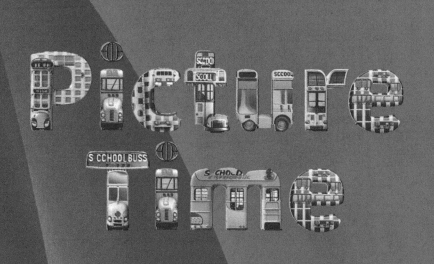

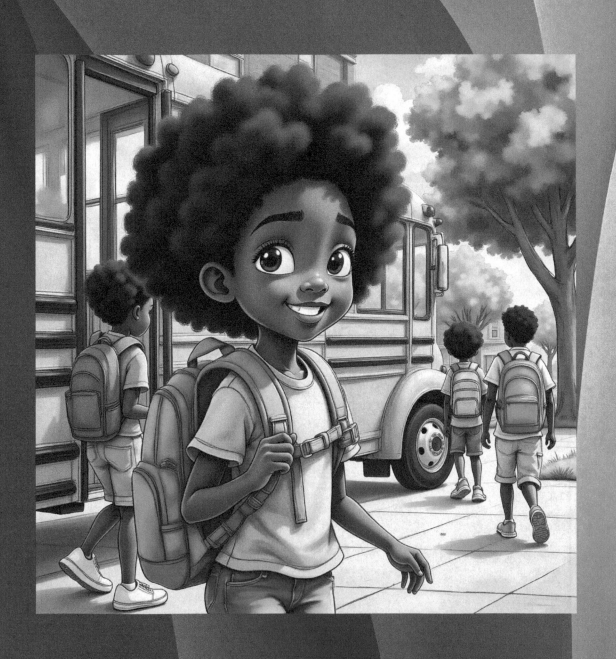

Children's books available on amazon.com Gloria Sanders-Williams covers many genres including fantasy, paranormal, and blank journals, so there is something to read for everyone.
www.Amazon.com/author/desire4fire
www.shadowandshade.com

Gloria
Sanders–Williams

Author's Books

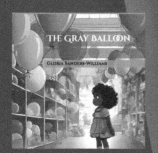

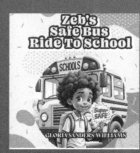

Made in United States
Orlando, FL
14 December 2024

55571297R00057